WITH A MOM *like mine*

WRITTEN BY CAROLYN MARRONE
ILLUSTRATED BY MARGARET POWER

"Hi Mom." I dropped my schoolbag on the floor and headed for the fridge.

"Not so fast, young man." My mother beckoned me back. "Unpack your bag first."

I sighed and unzipped my bag. I handed the school newsletter to Mom and put my lunchbox and thermos in the sink.

"This looks interesting," Mom said, looking up from the newsletter.

"What?" I asked. I never read the newsletter; it was usually full of stuff about lunch menus and things like that.

"This Saturday the fifth and sixth grade soccer team will play a match against a combined parent/teacher team," she read.

"All interested dads and moms are invited to take part."

"Oh," I said with a sinking feeling in my stomach. "That counts me out, then."

"It also says, 'All team members must attend,'" she said. "You're part of the team, Mike. That means you'll have to be there."

I looked down at the floor, biting my lip.

"Mike." She tilted my chin up so that I was forced to look at her. "I know how you're feeling," she said gently. "You're thinking that if your dad was still here, *he'd* be playing."

I shrugged, not trusting myself to speak. Although it was a month now since my father had left, I still couldn't believe he was really gone; didn't *want* to believe it, I suppose. Now this had cropped up, and the reality was looking me hard in the face.

"I'll tell you what," Mom said brightly. "It says dads *or* moms. Why don't I play?"

"No!" I said quickly, shaking my head. I hadn't told anyone at school that my father had gone, not even Phillip, my best friend. I'd tried to tell him a few times, but somehow the words just stuck in my throat. It was as if saying it out loud would make it real—and final. If my mother showed up at the game, *everyone* would know. "I'm sure none of the other kids' mothers will be playing," I said.

"Well—I might give Phillip's mother a call and see if she wants to be in it," Mom said. "I'm sure his dad won't be able to play, with his back so bad." She picked up the phone.

I sighed. Once Mom had made her mind up, there was no point in arguing. I just hoped Phillip's mother would say no; then perhaps Mom would give up on the idea.

I went into the living room and flopped into the beanbag in front of the television. I saw Mom glance toward me a couple of times as she talked, although I couldn't hear what she was saying. Then she hung up and came into the living room.

"It's all set," she said. "Phillip's mom said she'll play if I will."

"Oh, Mom!" I groaned.

"*Now* what's up?" she asked.

"It's just—no one would *expect* Phil's dad to be playing after his back operation and everything. But Dad—well—everyone knows what a great soccer player he is. If you come instead…" I spread my hands and shrugged.

She gave me a long look. "I gather you haven't told your friends that your father and I have separated."

I shook my head and gazed at the television.

"Mike." She reached over and turned the TV off, then sat on the floor in front of me. "Mike, you're not still counting on him coming back, are you?" She took hold of my hands. "You have to face the fact *some* time that he's gone for good."

I pulled my hands away and got up. "I have to do my homework," I muttered, blinking furiously to keep back the tears that prickled behind my eyes. She just didn't understand how I felt.

I hoped Mom would change her mind about the match, but on Saturday morning when she woke me up she was already dressed and ready to go; in Dad's old blue tracksuit, to make it even worse.

I got dressed slowly. Usually when I was going to play soccer, I couldn't get there quickly enough; but today I felt as if something heavy was weighing me down.

Mom chatted away happily as we drove to the field, but I sat scrunched down in my seat with my arms folded and didn't say a word.

When we arrived, we went up to Mr. Harvey, my teacher, who was acting as coach for the parent/teacher team.

"Glad you could make it, Mrs. Watson," he said. "I'm afraid we haven't had many parents show up." I clenched my teeth. That meant if Mom hadn't insisted on coming, no one would have even noticed anything odd about Dad not being there.

Phil and his mother came roaring up in their old bomb when it was almost time for the match to start; they were always late for everything.

"Come on Joan, I need some moral support here!" Mom called to Phil's mother. I felt my face color with embarrassment. As if it wasn't bad enough, without Mom drawing attention to herself!

The two of them went off to change. When they ran out on the field my shame was complete. Mom was wearing long, multi-colored striped socks and a pair of Dad's old soccer shorts. On top she wore a bright pink T-shirt with "SWEAT HOG" printed in big, black letters across the front. Around her head was a pink headband.

"Where'd you get that *shirt*?" I hissed as she jogged past me.

"Present from your Aunty Jean," she said over her shoulder. "Couldn't think of anywhere to wear it until now!"

She ran over to Mr. Harvey. "Hey Coach," she said, jogging up and down on the spot. "Where do you want me?" She gave him a hearty slap on the shoulder as she spoke.

I groaned to myself. All the other kids were grinning broadly.

Mr. Harvey looked a bit stunned. "Oh, er, I think right wing would be fine, Mrs. Watson," he said.

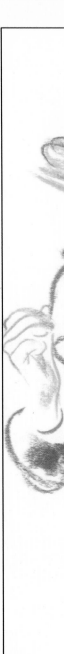

That was good, anyway—I was playing left fullback, so at least I wouldn't be anywhere near her.

The teacher who was refereeing blew the whistle and the game started.

It was a fairly even game. We were in better shape and used to playing together, but the grown-ups were stronger and a couple of the fathers were quite skillful.

At halftime the score was zero to zero. As we went off for the break I heard one of the boys say, "I thought Watson's old man would be playing."

I pretended not to hear, but my ears were burning.

In the second half we'd been playing for forty minutes and there was still no score.

Then my mother picked up a loose ball out on the wing and began to dribble it toward the goal. Steve Marwood, our star defender and team captain, went in to tackle her with a confident smile on his face. I could hardly believe my eyes when I saw Mom pull the ball back with her toe, tap it to the left, and dribble neatly around Steve before he even knew what happened.

Steve Marwood's father was right in front of the goal and calling for a pass. Mom crossed the ball high in the air— I didn't even know she could kick like that!

Mr. Marwood went for the header, but the ball sailed over his head, past our goalie, and into the corner of the net!

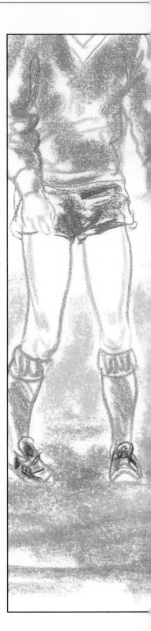

The teachers and the other kids' parents all cheered and ran up to Mom, patting her on the back and congratulating her. I felt all sort of mixed up inside; half proud and half annoyed.

When the final whistle blew, the score was still one to nothing, and they carried my mother off the field on their shoulders. When they finally put her down, she came over to me.

"Still mad at me?" she asked.

I shrugged. "I'll get over it," I said.

She put her hand on my shoulder. "I'm sorry if I've embarrassed you. But I had to make you see that from now on, *I* have to take the place of your father." She smiled. "If it comes to that, I felt a bit of a fool myself."

"Did you?" I asked in surprise.

She nodded, her face serious. "None of this has been all that easy for me either, you know."

I stared at her, suddenly ashamed. I'd been so busy feeling sorry for myself since Dad had left, I hadn't even *thought* about what it must be like for her.

"Mom, I..."

"Hey, Mrs. Watson!" Phil came bounding up. "That was a great goal!"

"Thanks, Phillip," Mom said. "But to tell the truth, I only meant it to be a pass."

"Well it was a great kick, anyway. My mom didn't even get a touch! How come you play soccer so well?"

Mom laughed. "I didn't follow Mike's dad for years around all those soccer matches without learning *something*," she said.

"Oh. Yeah." Phillip turned to me. "Er, sorry about, you know, your dad and everything," he mumbled, kicking the ground with the toe of his boot. "Mom told me last night."

I shrugged. "Don't worry about it," I said. For a moment I felt a lump rise in my throat. Then I grinned and slipped my arm through my mother's. With a Mom like mine, who needs a father?